POSH WATSON

Will shorts be glazzed-out tomorrow?
Are trumpet trainers just for bondos?
What's whirrabubble next?
Ask Posh Watson!

Gillian Cross has been writing children's books for more than fifteen years. She won the Carnegie Medal for her novel *Wolf* – and was a runner-up for the same award with *A Map of Nowhere*. *The Great Elephant Chase* won both the Whitbread Children's Novel Award and the Smarties Book Prize. Her other titles include *The Demon Headmaster* (recently shown as a serial on BBC Television) and *Beware Olga!* Married, with four children, her hobbies include orienteering and playing the piano.

Mike Gordon has illustrated many books for adults and children, including *Henry Hound* and *Hector the Spectre,* as well as greetings cards, books, mugs and T-shirts. He was named Berol Cartoonist of the Year in 1988.

Books by the same author

Beware Olga!
The Demon Headmaster
The Mintyglo Kid

For older readers

The Great Elephant Chase
Wolf

GILLIAN CROSS

POSH WATSON

Illustrations by Mike Gordon

WALKER BOOKS
AND SUBSIDIARIES
LONDON • BOSTON • SYDNEY

First published 1995 by
Walker Books Ltd, 87 Vauxhall Walk
London SE11 5HJ

This edition published 1996

2 4 6 8 10 9 7 5 3

Text © 1995 Gillian Cross
Illustrations © 1995 Mike Gordon

This book has been typeset in Garamond.

Printed in England

British Library Cataloguing in Publication Data
A catalogue record for this book
is available from the British Library.

ISBN 0-7445-4739-3

CONTENTS

CRUMBLE LANE

Crumble Lane School was dull. Not just a bit dull, like other schools, but so dull that even the spiders on the ceilings yawned.

The school uniform was grey, the classrooms were cold and bare, and all the teachers were as dull as dust. Especially Mrs Juniper, the Head. Her voice was so boring that everyone yawned every time she spoke.

The only person who was happy
at Crumble Lane was Natalie. That
was because she never took any
notice of Mrs Juniper.
She didn't care about
the teachers either,
or the classrooms.
She spent her whole
time sitting with a
heap of Maths sheets,
working away as
hard as she could.
She liked Maths
better than
anything else in
the world.

And every time she finished a sheet, her teacher took it away and stuck it up on the wall, as a decoration.

That's how boring Crumble Lane was.

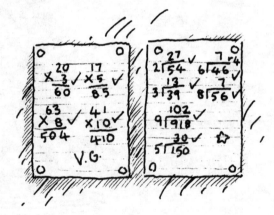

HOWDY-DOODLE-DO!

One dull Monday morning, Natalie
was tying her grey school tie round
the neck of her grey shirt when
there was a knock on the door.

Natalie opened the door – and almost fainted.

Outside was a boy in a purple jacket. He was wearing giant sunglasses and his hair stuck out all round his head, in bright yellow spikes.

He waved his lunch box at her. It was gold, and his initials sparkled in diamonds on the side.

"Hi, I'm Posh Watson," he said, "your new next door neighbour."

Natalie picked up her grey school coat, kissed her dad goodbye and stepped outside. "All right. Follow me," she said.

But Posh wasn't much good at following. For most of the way he was ahead of her, turning cartwheels along the pavement and waving at everyone in grey uniform. By the time they reached the school gates, there were twenty children following, all with their mouths open.

Mrs Juniper was standing in the playground with the bell in her hand. When she saw Posh, she almost dropped it. *Her* mouth fell open.

Posh cartwheeled straight up to her.

"I – er – " Mrs Juniper didn't know what to say. "Good morning."

Posh yawned. But Mrs Juniper didn't even notice. People always yawned when she spoke.

She rang the bell – and Posh stood on his hands and waggled his feet in her face.

Hoo-doodle-ray. Let's get inside and start the fun!

COPYING POSH

Natalie had a dreadful day.
Whenever she tried to settle down
with her Maths sheets, people came
up and poked her in the ribs.

All the children knew she was Posh's neighbour, and they thought she knew everything about him. They wouldn't leave her alone – even when she pulled faces and growled at them – because they wanted clothes like his.

By Tuesday, everyone else
seemed to be mad too. When Natalie
got to school, the playground was
full of peculiar clothes.

And everyone was yelling strange
words.

Natalie stood and stared. She
seemed to be the only person in
ordinary school uniform. Everyone
else was trying to be Posh Watson.
She looked round for the real Posh,
to see what he thought about it all.

But he wasn't there. Even when
Mrs Juniper came out to ring the
bell, there was no sign of him.

Or was there?

Suddenly, a Rolls Royce drew up outside the school and a very strange person stepped out of the back. He was wearing a long cloak and a black hat was pulled down over his hair. He came slinking through the gates and over to Natalie, just as Mrs Juniper rang the bell.

The strange person swept off his hat. It was Posh all right, but he looked quite, quite different.

Natalie blinked. "W-where's your purple jacket? And what about the spikes in your hair?"

"Do me a *favour*." Posh looked at
her, crushingly. "Spikes are out.
Only bondos have spikes in their
hair now."

"B-bondos?" Natalie said.

"That's right." Posh waved a hand
scornfully round the playground.

Only bondos are
still wearing spikes
and purple jackets.

Mrs Juniper rang the bell again,
and Posh stalked into school,
leaving everyone else muttering
behind him.

Natalie sighed. Today was going to be even worse than yesterday. She'd be lucky if she got any work done.

She was right. The moment she sat down in her corner at the back of the class, people began to creep up to her.

Mrs Juniper wasn't very happy, either. When they left school that afternoon, they found a notice stuck up on the school gate.

No purple coats!
No spiked hair!
BY ORDER
J. Juniper

BOOM-BA-BOOM!

There weren't any purple coats
or spiked hair at school on
Wednesday, but lots of people
came in black cloaks and hats with
feathers. The feathers got tangled
up, and the cloaks kept knocking
things over and catching on
splinters.

Natalie thought it was all Posh's
fault. But she couldn't say anything
because he wasn't there.

He didn't get to school until
playtime. And when he did, he
wasn't wearing a black cloak, or
a hat with a feather.

He came marching into the
playground in a pair of huge pink
trainers that played trumpet music
whenever he took a step.

And he wouldn't say anything
except:

Boom-ba-boom!

On Thursday, Posh was there early. When Natalie arrived, he was lying in the middle of the playground doing press-ups, in a T-shirt and a pair of running shorts. He had bare feet.

Natalie glared at him.

"Why aren't you wearing your trumpet-trainers?" she said crossly. "Everyone else is."

Posh jumped up and did a back flip. "Exactly! Musical shoes are glazzed-out."

"Glazzed-out?" Natalie said.

Glazzed right out. They're not whirrabubble.

Natalie groaned. She was having a dreadful week. By that afternoon, she'd done only two and a half Maths sheets, and the teacher didn't put those on the wall. All kinds of other things kept getting stuck up instead.

This school is
full of bondos
filling every room
Abso-doodle-utely
(Boom-ba-boom-ba-boom).

Whenever Natalie settled down to
work, people flicked notes at her
and hissed in her ear.

People kept trying to find out
what Posh was going to do *next*, so
that they wouldn't get left behind.
And they all thought Natalie knew,
because she was his neighbour.

She was having a miserable time.
So was Mrs Juniper.

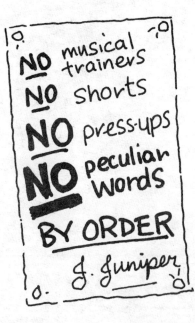

THIS HAS GOT TO STOP

On Friday morning, Natalie and
Posh walked to school together.
As they reached the gates, someone
pushed a note under Posh's nose.

Natalie looked at him. He was wearing a long earring, with a packet of chewing gum on the end, and a false moustache.

Natalie dragged Posh
up the corridor to Mrs
Juniper's office,
knocked on the
door and pushed
him in. He was still
cross, and he
grabbed hold of her
arm and
pulled her in too.

Mrs Juniper
looked at Posh.
She looked at the
earring and the
chewing gum and
the moustache.
And she frowned.

This has got to **stop!**

42

"The Inspectors are coming on Monday," she said. "Everyone's *got* to wear uniform."

She wrote a new notice.

Then she thought again, and wrote another one.

When she'd done that, she looked severely at Posh. "On Monday, I want to see you in a proper school uniform. Like Natalie."

"Like Natalie?" Posh looked at her and his eyes widened. "You mean – you want me to wear a skirt?"

"Of course not!" Mrs Juniper snapped. "I want you to wear Proper School Uniform. Like – like that." She pointed at last year's school photograph which was stuck up on her wall.

Posh stared at the rows of
children in neat, tidy uniform.

"But if you don't wear them, nobody else will," Mrs Juniper said. "There will be terrible trouble when the Inspectors come."

"I don't care about trouble," Posh said. "And I've got a really whizzaceous idea for Monday."

Mrs Juniper looked as if she were going to faint. "But everyone will copy you!"

Oh, dear! thought Natalie – and that was when she had her brainwave.

She looked at Mrs Juniper. She looked at Posh. She thought about the Inspectors. Then, in a very small voice, she said, "I've got a *really* whizzaceous idea. If you do what I say, you can both have what you want…"

THE INSPECTORS

On Monday, Natalie got up early. She dressed as usual, in her school uniform – grey skirt, grey shirt, grey tie. Then she ran downstairs and phoned Samantha, the school gossip.

Then she had her breakfast and
walked to school with her fingers
crossed.

At five to nine, the Inspectors
arrived in their big black cars. They
looked out over the playground. All
the children were in neat school
uniform. Even Posh Watson.

Yawn! Yawn!

Yawn!

Natalie went up to them.

The Inspectors nodded, and
yawned even harder. Natalie knew
just what they were thinking. *This
school is even duller than last time
we came.* She crossed her fingers
again and led them into the hall.

They sat up on the platform,
yawning as the children walked in.

They looked very bored.

When all the children were
sitting down, there was a most
extraordinary noise at the back of
the hall.

TARA-TARA-TARA!
BOOM-BA-
BOOM!

And in came the teachers!

Every teacher was wearing
something wild and strange and
weird. And
behind them
all, dancing
and prancing up
the middle of
the hall, came
someone Natalie
hardly recognized –
Mrs Juniper!
She bounded on to
the stage, beamed at
the Inspectors and
held out her hand.

The Inspectors sat up straight and
their eyes opened wide. They
weren't yawning any more. And
they didn't yawn when Mrs Juniper
showed them round the school.

They were too busy looking at
the pictures on the walls.

At the neat, tidy children.

And the wild, weird teachers.

And the amazing, energetic Head
– Mrs Jumping Juniper.

Mrs Jumping Juniper was so
happy she was actually smiling.
She'd got what she wanted at last.

Posh was smiling too. Because *everyone* had copied him now – even the teachers.

But the happiest person in the
whole school was sitting in a corner
all by herself. Nobody was
bothering her –

and she was having
a wonderful time.

MORE WALKER SPRINTERS
For You to Enjoy